A MOUSE'S TALE

BY PAMELA JOHNSON

Harcourt Brace & Company

SAN DIEGO   NEW YORK   LONDON

Library of Congress Cataloging-in-Publication Data
Johnson, Pamela.
A mouse's tale/by Pamela Johnson. — 1st ed.
p. cm.
Summary: A mouse who longs to travel by sea considers and discards
various boating options before creating her own mouse-sized vessel out of
things she finds on the beach.
ISBN 0-15-256032-7
[1. Mice — Fiction. 2. Boats and boating — Fiction.] I. Title.
PZ7.J6353Mo   1991
[E] — dc20   90-36805

B C D E F

Printed in Singapore

The illustrations in this book were done in colored pencil
on watercolor paper.
The display type was set in Caslon Open Face.
The text type was set in Primer.
Composition by Thompson Type, San Diego, California
Color separations were made by Bright Arts, Ltd., Singapore.
Printed and bound by Tien Wah Press, Singapore
Production supervision by Warren Wallerstein and Michele Green
Designed by Martha Roach

In a large marsh near the sea there once lived a small but adventuresome mouse. Every day in each season, the little mouse wandered through the grasses, over the dunes to the sea, where she stood gazing at the water.

The mouse longed to travel upon the waves, and she dreamed of wonderful ships that would carry her far and wide.

She imagined she would like to travel aboard a magnificent ocean liner.

But in such an enormous ship, she thought, how would I feel the soft spray of the sea?

"Perhaps something smaller would be better," said the mouse.

One night the mouse saw a ferryboat strung with dazzling lights. The noise of the ferry, the music and laughter, danced across the water, all the way to shore where the mouse stood.

How she wished to ride the ferry! But, she wondered, would so much gaiety drown the cries of sea gulls and the lapping of the waves that I love to hear?

Perhaps something quieter than a ferryboat, thought the little mouse.

A tugboat, she mused; tugboats come in bright colors, and they are very useful.

"But, oh — their stacks blow thick black smoke and spread soot all day and night! How would I see the sun or the stars?"

Perhaps something cleaner would be better, thought the mouse. And she sighed like a tiny wave.

"Of course," said the mouse aloud. "Of course! A fishing boat with fine nets will do."

But the smell, she thought. I would smell nothing but fish, fish, fish, instead of the fresh, salty air that I love.

"No, not a fishing boat," she decided. "A fishing boat is not what I want."

What I require is much simpler, much quieter, much cleaner, thought the mouse.

"Perhaps a dinghy with one comfortable seat and a pair of smooth wooden oars," she said.

The mouse paused again and considered. "I would have to row and row, very hard and long indeed, to go as far as I want to go. I would be too tired to feel anything more than the ache in my arms.

"Oh, what shall I do?" she asked in despair.

The mouse walked thoughtfully along the beach. Her head drooped; her tail dragged sadly behind her in the damp sand.

"How can I go to sea?"

The little mouse wandered among the litter of seaweed, smooth stones, and shells. And because she was sad, and not minding her steps, she nearly tangled herself in a long, sturdy strand of eel grass.

This might be of use some day, thought the mouse. Not paying much attention, she coiled the grass in a loop like a rope.

The waves grew smaller and gentler as the tide ran out. In front of the mouse, a gull's feather lifted itself like a small sail puffed with wind.

The mouse thought, I will take this feather with me, too, because it is so lovely and white, just like a sail.

The mouse sighed again and looked into a tiny pool left by the outgoing tide. Half-covered by water, but already beginning to dry, was a small, pink crab's claw, shaped like a sailboat tiller.

The mouse fished the claw from the water and, unheeding, added it to her pile of beachcombings.

As the mouse turned away from the tide
pool, she nearly tumbled into a large shell.
It was twice her size but very light. It
rocked back and forth when she nudged it.

The mouse dropped the coil of grass, the
feather, and the claw beside the teetering
shell. She climbed onto the shelf that covered
almost half the shell. She stared at the sea,
thinking very hard about ships and boats.

Suddenly, with a glance toward the turning tide, she began to work in a great flurry.

Gnawing here and there through the length of eel grass, poking and tying, she fastened the claw to one end of the shell.

Then she lashed the quill of the feather to a small hole in the shell's seat.

The mouse scurried about to examine her handiwork. Then, just as the sea began to creep toward the shell, she hopped aboard.

The water rose all around her, and soon the shell was afloat. It moved without purpose until the mouse pulled on the lines and tugged at the tiller.

She sailed. The feather held the breeze and the shell moved gently through the water.

The mouse sniffed the salt air. She felt the waves' gentle spray on her whiskers. Overhead, sea gulls clamored and called.

"Oh, at last!" cried the mouse as she sailed toward the sun. "At last I'm going to sea."